POLAR OPPOSITES

Written and
illustrated by
Erik Brooks

Marshall Cavendish Children

Text and illustrations copyright © 2010 by Erik Brooks

Marshall Cavendish Corporation
99 White Plains Road
Tarrytown, NY 10591
www.marshallcavendish.us/kids

Library of Congress Cataloging-in-Publication Data
Brooks, Erik
Polar opposites / by Erik Brooks. — 1st ed.
p. cm.
Summary: Alex, a polar bear, and Zina, a penguin, are very different but they can still find ways to meet in the middle.
ISBN 978-0-7614-5685-8
[1. Individuality—Fiction. 2. Polar bear—Fiction. 3. Bears—Fiction. 4.
Penguins—Fiction. 5. Polar regions—Fiction.] I. Title.
PZ7.B7935Po 2010
[E]—dc22
2009005214

The illustrations are rendered in pencil, charcoal, and watercolor.
Editor: Robin Benjamin

Printed in Malaysia (T)
First edition
10 9 8 7 6 5 4 3 2 1

 Marshall Cavendish
Children

For Steve,
and for complementary
opposites around the world

 lex is a **BIG** polar bear.

Zina is a tiny **penguin**.

Alex and Zina are
polar opposites!

Equator

They live on opposite
sides of the world.

Alex lives in the Arctic.

Zina lives in the Antarctic.

Alex is mostly white, with some black.

Zina is mostly black, with some white.

Alex is shaggy.

Zina is smooth.

Polar opposites are different . . .

. . . in SO many ways!

Alex gets up late.

Zina rises early.

Alex likes sour things.

Zina likes sweet things.

Alex is messy.

Zina is neat.

Alex is loud.

Zina is quiet. *Shhh.* . . .

Alex's favorite clothes are bright.

Zina's favorites are not.

Alex pushes.

Zina pulls.

Alex travels fast!

Zina takes it slow.

Alex and Zina are *very* different.

But even polar opposites . . .

. . . can ALWAYS meet in the middle!

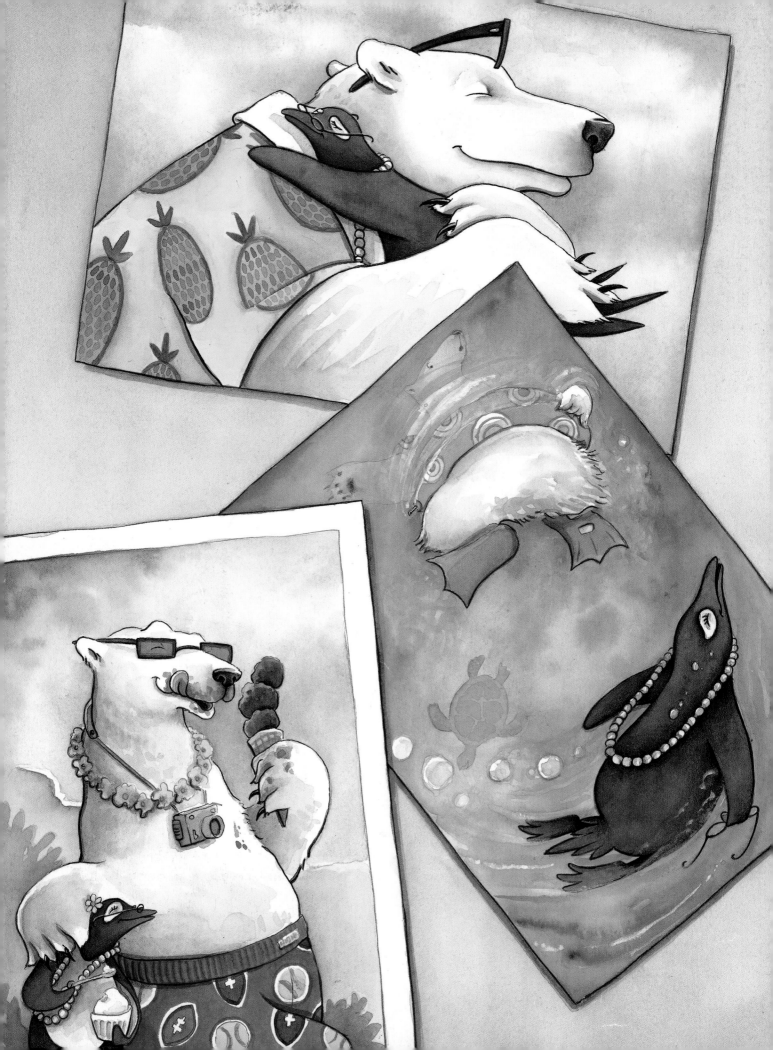

Alex and Zina

Galapagos Islands
June 2010

See you next year!